W9-CDJ-476

For Miss Talbert, Miss Zilka, and Miss Hatt, who taught *me* how to grow candy

ACKNOWLEDGMENTS

I would like to thank April Stevens and Sara Stevens for their brilliant suggestions. I would like to thank Kevin Fisher, Barbara Ensor, and Andy Barnet for their advice and encouragement. I would like to thank Karen Hatt for sharing her confectionary knack. I would like to thank Aidan for his creative and inventive solutions. I would like to thank Olive for her inspirational love of candy and for not eating Ruby's garden. And finally, I would like to thank Anne Schwartz and Lee Wade for their extraordinary patience, keen insight, and sugarcoated revisions.

Published in the United States by Schwartz & Wade Books, an imprint of Random House Children's Books, a division of Random House, Inc., New York.
Schwartz & Wade Books and colophon are trademarks of Random House, Inc.
www.randomhouse.com/kids
Educators and librarians, for a variety of teaching tools, visit us at
www.randomhouse.com/teachers
Library of Congress Cataloging-in-Publication Data
Fisher, Valorie.
When Ruby tried to grow candy / Valorie Fisher.
— 1st ed p. cm.
Summary: After meeting her mysterious neighbor, a young girl plants a candy garden, with delicious results.
ISBN 978-0-375-84015-9 (alk. paper) –
ISBN 978-0-375-94015-6 (lib. bdg.)
[1. Candy—Fiction. 2. Neighbors—Fiction. 3. Gardening—Fiction.] I. Title. PZ7.F53485Wh 2008 [E]—dc22
2006102106
PRINTED IN CHINA
1 3 5 7 9 10 8 6 4 2
First Edition

when ruby tried to grow candy

VALORIE FISHER

a schwartz & wade book · new york

Ruby Louise Hawthorn lived in a charming house on a quiet street where everything was perfectly perfect—except for one thing.

And that was the lady next door.

"She's perfectly pleasant. Leave her alone," Ruby's mother always said.

But Ruby knew better. She'd heard the weird noises and crazy cackles. She was sure something monstrous and mean lurked behind that big fence.

Thump, thump, thump.

"Rubeeeeee, don't bounce the ball against the fence!" her mother hollered from the house. So Ruby tossed her ball into the air instead.

And in the blink of an eye, Ruby Louise Hawthorn
had tossed herself into quite a pickle.

Ruby dashed to the potting shed and bumbled back.

In a flash, she scribbled a note, scrambled over the fence . . .

In the likely event I never return, tell miss Myrtle that I didn't finish my homework because I perished, and tell Fern that she can have my jumprope if it hasn't perished with me.
signed,
Ruby Louise Hawthorn
500 REGULAR LENGTH No. 1
QUALITY SEED
HIGHEST GRADE
CEN. SCI. CO.

. . . and plopped down right in front of a peculiar little lady.

"My b-b-b-b-ball, I lost it," stuttered Ruby.

"My plants, you squished them," the lady grumbled. "And who are you?"

"Ruby Louise Hawthorn," said Ruby.

"Miss Wysterious." The lady introduced herself. "Was it a red ball with pink dots?"

"Yes!" said Ruby.

"I haven't seen it."

Ruby glanced around. "Why are teacups hanging on your tree?" she asked.

"My teacups aren't hanging, they're growing," Miss Wysterious snarled.

"You grew a teacup?" asked Ruby. "How?"

"The usual way—with water, sunshine, and the occasional chitchat," explained Miss Wysterious.

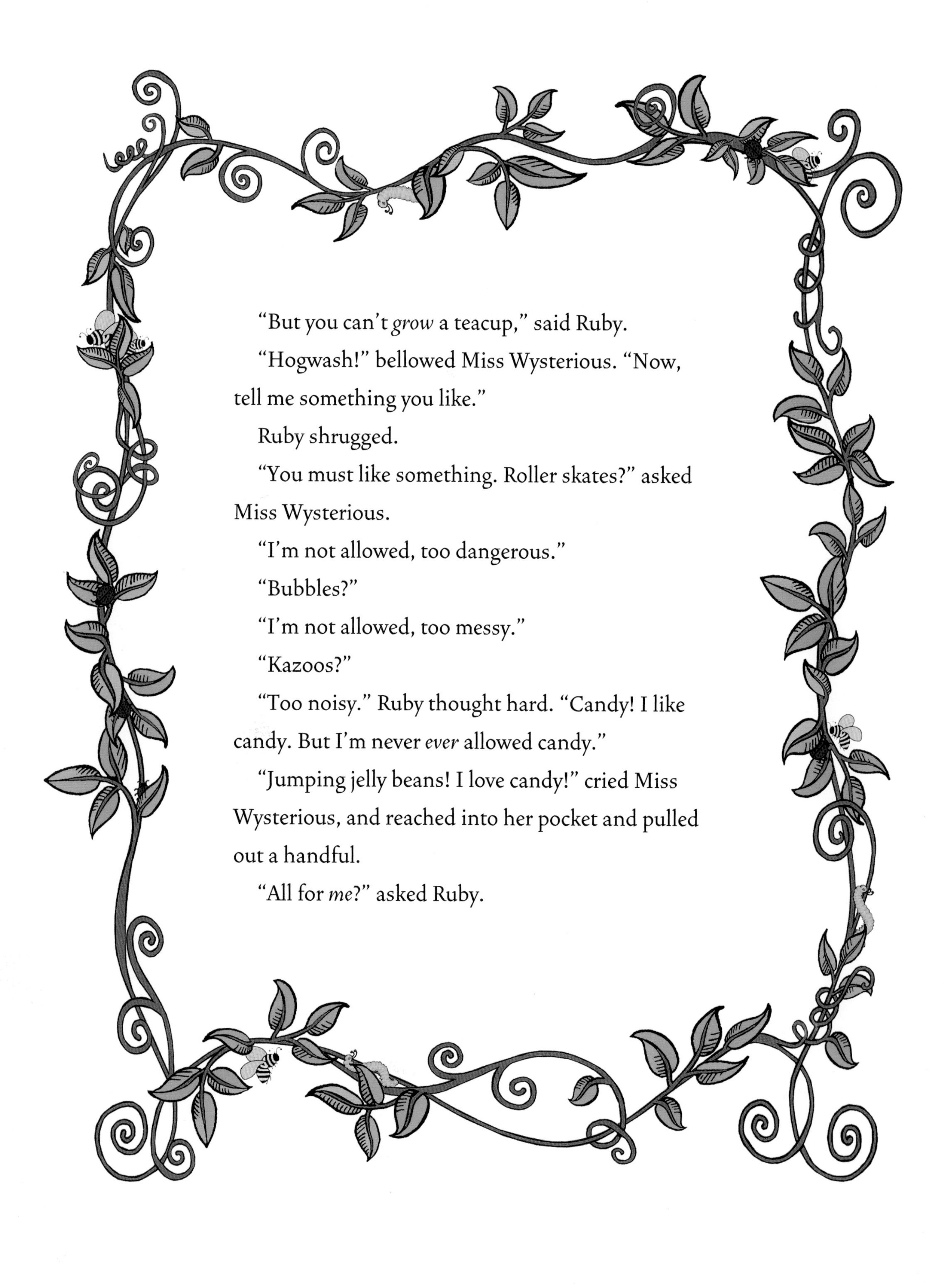

"But you can't *grow* a teacup," said Ruby.

"Hogwash!" bellowed Miss Wysterious. "Now, tell me something you like."

Ruby shrugged.

"You must like something. Roller skates?" asked Miss Wysterious.

"I'm not allowed, too dangerous."

"Bubbles?"

"I'm not allowed, too messy."

"Kazoos?"

"Too noisy." Ruby thought hard. "Candy! I like candy. But I'm never *ever* allowed candy."

"Jumping jelly beans! I love candy!" cried Miss Wysterious, and reached into her pocket and pulled out a handful.

"All for *me*?" asked Ruby.

"Don't be ridiculous. Turn the soil over, plant them one inch deep and six inches apart, and give them plenty of water. Now move it!" Miss Wysterious barked, and she scurried away.

Ruby popped a jelly bean into her mouth. It was marvelous. It was extraordinary. It was divine.

She planted one lemon sour, and gobbled one. She planted one toffee, and gobbled two. She planted one butterscotch, and gobbled three.

Ruby planted and gobbled, until all the candy was gone.

"I'm done," said Ruby.

"Then come back tomorrow to water," said Miss Wysterious.

"But they'll never grow," said Ruby.

"If you're in doubt, nothing will sprout," snapped Miss Wysterious, and off she dashed.

Well, Ruby was sure of one thing: Miss Wysterious's candy was irresistible.

The next day, Ruby decided that just in case, maybe, perhaps, she would water just once.

lemon sours
butterscotch
gumdrops
jellybeans

And Ruby watered once, a few times, just in case.

"Nothing is growing," said Ruby after a week of watering.

"It doesn't always work," confessed Miss Wysterious. "Socks, for instance. Shoes grow like weeds, but I've never been able to sprout a sock."

weeds
keep out!

Over the next few weeks, Miss Wysterious babbled to her plants and rattled off tips for Ruby. "Plant with a plan, Hawthorn, never willy-nilly. Shorter plants in front of the taller ones—gives them all plenty of sunshine. Now move along!"

Ruby buzzed about the garden all that day,

and the next day,

and the days after that.

"Always pick eggbeaters before a storm. Otherwise, when the wind blows, the din is deafening. And buttons must be picked early, unless you need them the size of frying pans! And remember, with shoes always plant a pair." Miss Wysterious shook her head. "Heaven knows what I'll do with all these left shoes!

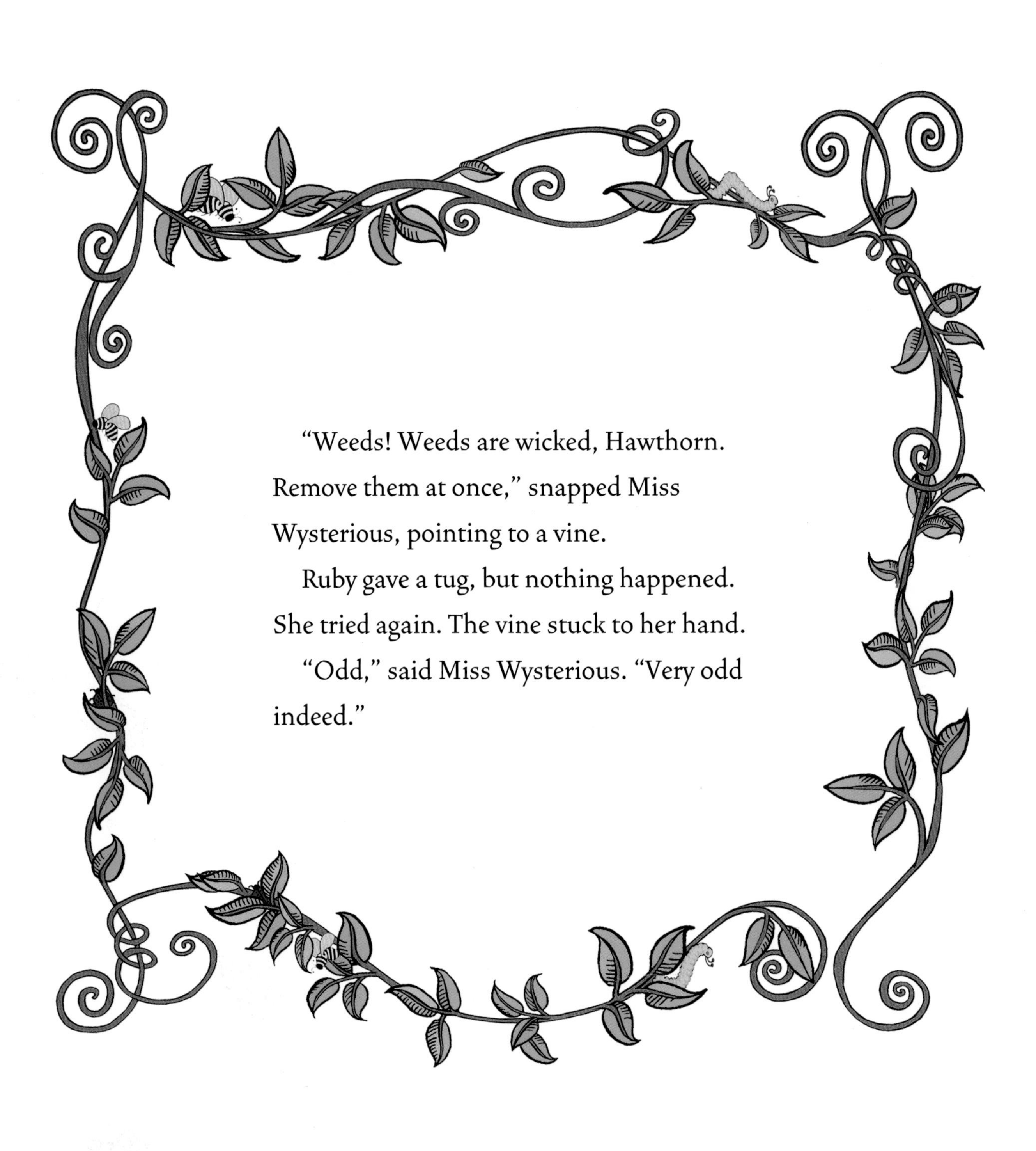

"Weeds! Weeds are wicked, Hawthorn. Remove them at once," snapped Miss Wysterious, pointing to a vine.

Ruby gave a tug, but nothing happened. She tried again. The vine stuck to her hand.

"Odd," said Miss Wysterious. "Very odd indeed."

Together Ruby and Miss Wysterious followed the curious vine as it twisted, and turned, and twirled all around the garden.

"Blazing butterscotch, Hawthorn, look what you've grown!" exclaimed Miss Wysterious.
Ruby gasped in astonishment. All around her were the most remarkable plants she had ever seen.

Ruby licked a leaf. She chewed a petal. She nibbled a bud. It was the sweetest, most scrumptiously delicious stuff she had ever tasted.

Lickety-split, Ruby polished off a peppermint blossom while Miss Wysterious gobbled up some gumdrops.

"Seems you have a sweet tooth *and* a green thumb," chuckled Miss Wysterious. "Now, what in thundering toffee are you going to do with all this?"

Ruby flashed a smile. "Don't worry. I know *just* what to do."

yo-yos
finger paint

And the very next day Ruby got to work in her own backyard, planting just a few of her favorite things.